# Bad Weekend

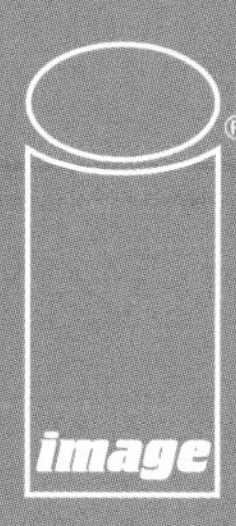



BAD WEEKEND, July 2019. First printing.
Contains material originally published in magazine form as CRIMINAL #2-3.
Published by Image Comics, Inc. Office of publication: 2701 NW Vaughn St., Suite 780, Portland, OR 97210.
 ISBN: 978-1-5343-1440-5.

Publication design by Sean Phillips

# Bad Weekend

a CRIMINAL novella by

**Ed Brubaker**
**Sean Phillips**

Colors by Jacob Phillips

July, 1997
I was out doing footwork on a job I was having trouble with...

And when I came home there was a message on my machine.

HI JACOB... IT'S MINDY, FROM THE CONVENTION.
COMIC FEST, I MEAN.
COULD YOU GIVE ME A CALL BACK, PLEASE? IT'S KIND OF URGENT.
??

Apparently, Hal Crane was flying in to be given a Lifetime Achievement Award and they needed someone to... uh... basically be his minder for a few days. Make sure he got to the ceremony and his other appearances.
...I DON'T KNOW... I'VE GOT A LOT GOING ON...
PLEASE... IT'S JUST FOR THE WEEKEND...
HE ASKED FOR YOU SPECIFICALLY, JACOB.

Right after high school, about ten years before this, I was one of Hal's **assistants**.
He went through three or four of them a year back then, and I guess I lasted longer than most...
But it ended badly with us.

Of course, that didn't make me special. Hal ended most of his relationships badly.

Supposedly, when he quit working for ***National*** back in the day, he decked Julie Schwartz over a bad inking job...

And there's another story about him pulling a gun on some editor at Marvel in the early '70s... Gerry Conway, I think.

Hal said all that stuff was bullshit, that all he ever did was yell and throw some things around a few times...
WHY WOULD HE ASK FOR ***ME?***
I HAVEN'T ***HEARD*** FROM HIM SINCE I QUIT.
I DON'T KNOW, HE JUST ***DID***...

...But you still hear lots of those stories, and no one has any trouble *believing* them.
I sure didn't.
LOOK, HE GETS HERE FRIDAY MORNING... WHAT CAN I DO TO PERSUADE YOU?
A *LIFETIME PASS* TO THE FEST?
TO MY PAL JACOB -Hal Crane '88

In my experience, Hal Crane was a collection of bad habits and worse moods...

But somewhere under all the smoke and whiskey and sullen glares was one of the most talented artists you ever saw.

The kind of guy who could ink with a toothbrush or a broken stick and the page would still come out perfect.

Which is why everyone put up with everything else about him...
And why I said -
OKAY, I GUESS I'LL DO IT.
I was a sucker for Hal's punishment, because I was probably his biggest fan.
TO MY PAL JACOB -Hal Crane '88

Friday

I realize I'm acting like you know who Hal Crane is, when you probably don't...
Unless you know a lot about comics.

But there are two reasons you might have heard of Hal anyway...

Things that had made him ***kind of*** famous in the "real" world.

First, because he was the main design and storyboard artist for ***DANNY DAGGER AND THE FANTASTICALS***, a cartoon my generation grew up with.
DANNY DAGGER
And The
FANTASTICALS
Copyright ©1967 Harmony-Gems

***Danny Dagger***, ***Princess Yaz***, her little brother ***Tanner*** and his pet dragon ***Stuffy*** were not huge hits when they originally aired...
But the afterschool reruns in the '70s had made the show a pop culture sensation... Syndicated and merchandised around the world.
for MORE !
4 OCT' '67
"DANNY DAGGER and the FANTASICALS"
FANTASICALS"
©1967-HarmonyGems

This is not something you want to bring up with Hal Crane if you ever meet him, by the way.
He hated that show, even before he felt ripped off by it.

So it's kind of funny that when I finally spot Hal across the hotel lobby, he's talking to a woman in a **Princess Yaz** costume.
And he's actually smiling and being polite, too.

For a second I wonder if he's changed... maybe gotten sober or found God...

But then she slaps him...

And I laugh at myself for thinking anything would be different.
JESUS...

HEY, ***KID***... IT'S GOOD TO SEE YOU.
WHAT THE HELL WAS ***THAT*** ABOUT?

AH... NOTHING...
I OFFERED HER A HUNDRED BUCKS TO COME UP TO MY ROOM.
JESUS, HAL - YOU CAN'T DO STUFF LIKE THAT.

I THOUGHT SHE WAS A PROSTITUTE.
WHY?

SHE'S A BOOTH BABE. AREN'T THEY ALL -
SHE'S NOT A BOOTH BABE, HAL.

SHE'S A FAN.
SHE PROBABLY MADE THAT COSTUME HERSELF.

GIRLS COME TO THIS CON DRESSED LIKE THAT AND NO ONE'S PAYING THEM?
YEAH.

WHY?

BECAUSE IT'S NOT 1978 ANYMORE.
NOW COME ON... LET'S GO GET YOUR SCHEDULE...

WHY IS THIS PLACE SO *CROWDED?*
I THOUGHT COMICS WAS GOING *BUST?*

OH... I DON'T KNOW...
I DON'T REALLY KEEP UP WITH THE *FAN PRESS* ANYMORE.

Hal was right, though. This was 1997 and the comics industry was in a death spiral.
Publishers going bankrupt, distributors imploding, shops closing all over the country.
Comics was a tiny business that was going down for the last time and everybody knew it.

But the convention hall was more crowded than ever, everyone all smiling and happy.
Maybe no one had told them the party was ending soon.

Or maybe they were here for the last hurrah.
True fans will always go down with the ship.

It's one of their best and worst qualities.

SO... LOOKS LIKE YOU'VE GOT A PANEL COMING UP...
IT'S YOU... JOE KUBERT... WILL EISNER AND AL WILLIAMSON.
OH YEAH, THE OLD-TIMERS PANEL...
I'M NOT GOING TO THAT.

YOU'RE JUST GONNA NOT SHOW UP?
I'M SURE NO ONE'LL MISS ME.

YES, THEY WILL. THE ORGANIZERS ARE GONNA BE PISSED.
WELL, TOO BAD... BECAUSE WE GOT OTHER PLANS.

SHIT... WE'RE LATE ALREADY.

I said there were *two reasons* you might know Hal Crane's name.
And the second one is why he's sitting in the back seat, like I'm his chauffeur.

Hal was the other person in the car with *Archie Lewis* when he crashed in 1955.
CRASH KILL STAR KING ARTOONIST

It's one of comics' famous deaths, like Max Gaines or Jack Cole or Wally Wood.
The police ruled it an accident, but the rumors that Lewis was suicidal have never gone away.
KING
Archie Lewis

Hal had been inking backgrounds on *STAR KING* for a few months before the crash.

He was just a kid starting to make a name for himself...

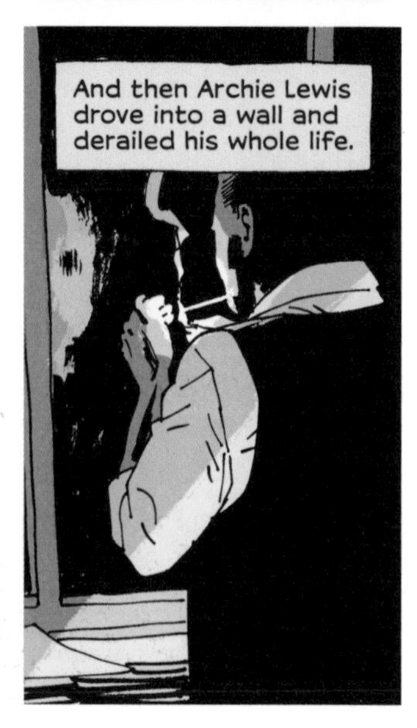
And then Archie Lewis drove into a wall and derailed his whole life.

I remember talking to Joe Orlando once about Hal back in those days...
And he said before that wreck, Hal was the sweetest guy you ever met. Just this talented kid bursting with ideas.

The cantankerous Hal, the paranoid and bitter one, the drunk... That came later.
BAR

That car crash is another thing you should ***never*** mention to Hal, obviously.

I've actually only heard him talk about it one time...
***HERE*** HE IS... THANK GOD.

...That day in the car, when his idol died and he walked away with barely a scratch.
THOUGHT MAYBE YOU WERE CHANGING YOUR MIND, HAL.
NO... NOT IF YOU BROUGHT THE ***CASH***.

THESE LOOK LEGIT, RIGHT?
ME AND MY BUDDY MADE 'EM AT THIS COPY SHOP HE WORKS AT, AFTER HOURS.

YEAH, THEY LOOK PRETTY CLOSE TO THE REAL THING.

COUNTERFEIT ANIMATION CELS...
HOW MUCH ARE YOU GETTING FOR THESE?
ABOUT THREE HUNDRED EACH...
AND THEY MOVE FAST WITH HAL'S SIGNATURE.

BUT DON'T WORRY, MAN, I'M KEEPING 'EM UNDER THE TABLE...
FOR "SERIOUS COLLECTORS" ONLY.
GOOD... YOU DON'T WANT TO LET THE STUDIO LAWYERS SEE THAT STUFF.

These skeevy art dealer types were always circling Hal like vultures.

And he always needed their money -- usually to pay off gambling debts when I worked for him.
I think he hated these guys as much as he hated his publishers...
Since he'd sold off all his best pages years ago, then watched them sell over and over again for higher prices.

It was sad, but Hal had done it to himself.
No one forced him to go to the racetrack or have three ex-wives.

HEY DICK... YOU HEAR ABOUT ANY OF MY STUFF GOING ON THE MARKET RECENTLY?
UH... THERE WAS THAT PRINCESS YAZ CHARACTER SHEET LAST MONTH...

NO... THIS WOULD BE A BIGGER DEAL THAN THAT...

I DON'T KNOW, MAN...
WITH THE NEW SHOW COMING UP, PRINCESS YAZ IS A PRETTY BIG DEAL NOW.

WHAT NEW SHOW?

SOME LIVE ACTION THING... NO DANNY DAGGER, JUST PRINCESS YAZ...
IT'S LIKE... GIRL POWER OR WHATEVER...

WHY DIDN'T YOU TELL ME ABOUT THIS?
BECAUSE I DIDN'T KNOW.

OH... IT'S NOT OFFICIAL YET, BUT PEOPLE HAVE BEEN TALKING...
WORD IS THEY'RE ANNOUNCING SOON... MAYBE THIS WEEKEND AT THE FEST.
WELL... ISN'T THAT JUST GREAT...

BUT I WAS ACTUALLY TALKING ABOUT OLDER PAGES... RARE STUFF...

YOU WANT ME TO ASK AROUND? I COULD GIVE SCOTT A CALL...
NO, THAT'S ALL RIGHT...

...DON'T WORRY ABOUT IT.

Frank Harmony was the co-founder of the animation studio Hal worked at...

The guy who got rich off *Danny Dagger*.

Hal decides he wants a nap back at his hotel, and then maybe he'll consider the dinner.
Heavy emphasis on the *"maybe"* in that sentence.
But he doesn't count on the persistence of the convention staff...
HAL!! THERE YOU ARE!

OH, HEY MINDY... I WAS JUST --
YOU MISSED YOUR PANEL... AND YOU HAVE A SIGNING THAT STARTED TEN MINUTES AGO.
OH, I... UH.
JACOB, DIDN'T YOU SEE THAT ON HIS SCHEDULE?

IT'S AT THE BOTTOM OF THE PANEL LISTING, SEE - "SIGNING AFTER PANEL."
SHIT. I TOTALLY MISSED THAT.
WELL, IT'S A GOOD THING I CAME OVER HERE, THEN... ISN'T IT?

I can tell Hal wants to run for it, but Mindy's too much a force of nature...
COME ON, HAL... LET'S GO.

And it's my first smile of the weekend.
THERE ARE FANS IN LINE WAITING FOR YOU.

It doesn't last long.
ARE YOU KIDDING ME...?
MEET HAL CRANE ARTIST OF DANNY DANGER!
Convention Guest

...ONE GUY?
I SWEAR TO GOD THERE WAS A WHOLE LINE OF PEOPLE HERE BEFORE.

LOOK - JUST SIT... OKAY?
I'LL GO MAKE AN ANNOUNCEMENT ON THE LOUDSPEAKERS.

TRUST ME, PEOPLE WILL SHOW UP WHEN THEY KNOW YOU'RE HERE.
THEY *BETTER*.

AND I'LL SEE YOU AT THE *DINNER* AFTER THIS, *RIGHT?*
YEAH... OF COURSE.

SO NOW YOU *DO* WANT TO GO TO THE DINNER?
*NO*... BUT I'M NOT GONNA TELL *HER* THAT...
I'M A NICE GUY.

MR CRANE, IT'S *SUCH* AN *HONOR* TO MEET YOU.
I'VE BEEN A FAN SINCE... WELL, MY *WHOLE LIFE.*

GREAT.
IS THERE SOMETHING YOU WANT ME TO *SIGN?*

OH, UH... JUST THIS...

...IF THAT'S OKAY...?
DANNY DAGGER And The FANTASTICALS

NO PROBLEM.

ANYTHING ELSE?
NO, BUT... ARE YOU GOING TO BE DOING SKETCHES?

NO... NO SKETCHING. I'VE GOT ARTHRITIS.
OH... OKAY...

NICE TO MEET YOU.

YOU SHOULD TRY MAKING EYE CONTACT WITH A FAN ONCE IN A WHILE.
OR MAYBE EVEN SMILE.
AHH... SCREW HIM...
HE'S GONNA SELL THAT LUNCHBOX TWO ROWS OVER AND YOU KNOW IT.
Back in the old days, Hal didn't care about stuff like that.

He'd sit doing sketches for hours, with fans crowding around to watch him work...
Laughing at all his jokes.
Hal says he always hated the convention scene, but I don't believe it...

There's no way he doesn't miss those days.
HEY, MR CRANE...
I'M CRAIG FROOP FROM THE COMICS REVIEW.

I WAS WONDERING IF WE COULD DO A QUICK INTERVIEW?
ABOUT WHAT?

WELL... YOUR WHOLE CAREER...
I MEAN, YOU'VE BEEN IN THE TRENCHES FOREVER...

YOU CAME IN WHEN HORROR AND SCI-FI WERE ON TOP...
...AND YOU SURVIVED WHEN THE SUPERHEROES CAME BACK, TOO.

WE COULD START THERE...
LIKE, I ALWAYS HEARD YOU HATED DRAWING SUPERHEROES.
OH, I DON'T KNOW IF I'D SAY THAT.

BUT YOU HAD MORE FUN ON THE SWORD-AND-SORCERY BOOKS, RIGHT?
YOUR RUN ON ZANGAR BACK IN '79? ALL THAT HIGH ADVENTURE STUFF.
I DON'T KNOW... MAYBE.

AND DIDN'T YOU START OUT TRYING TO BE A NEWSPAPER STRIP GUY?

I THINK SOMEONE TOLD ME THAT.

LISTEN, KID... I'M NOT REALLY IN THE MOOD FOR THIS RIGHT NOW.

IF YOU WANT TO SCHEDULE TIME TO DO A PROPER INTERVIEW, TALK TO MY ASSISTANT.
SERIOUSLY?

YES... YOU DON'T JUST WALK UP AND SHOVE A TAPE RECORDER IN A MAN'S FACE.
THAT'S NOT HOW THINGS ARE DONE.

OH, WHATEVER... I WAS JUST TRYING TO GIVE YOU SOME FREE PRESS...
YOU DON'T HAVE TO BE A DICK ABOUT IT.
Convention Guest

THAT WASN'T MY FAULT.
I DIDN'T SAY ANYTHING.

HEY... MISTER...?

GO AHEAD, TOMMY, ASK HIM.
WILL YOU... OTTER-GRAPH...
...MY BOOKLET...?

SURE, KID...
THANKS.
MEET HAL CRANE

YOU CAN JUST SIGN IT ON THE COVER...

...ANYWHERE'S GOOD.
Comic Fest '97
THE IMAGE REVOLUTION IS HERE!

HERE YOU GO.
THANK YOU!

GET ME THE FUCK OUT OF HERE.
OKAY.

YOU ALL RIGHT?
I JUST NEED A DRINK...

ATTENTION IN THE MAIN HALL... LEGENDARY ARTIST HAL CRANE, CREATOR OF DANNY DAGGER, IS NOW SIGNING AT BOOTH 27-D...

We end up in the bar where all the comics pros come to drink at these things. Waiting for the old friends he actually ***wants*** to see, Hal says.
HEY KID... WHY DIDN'T YOU BRING ANY OF YOUR RECENT PAGES TO SHOW ME?
I DON'T REALLY ***HAVE*** ANY RECENT PAGES, HAL.
I'VE GOT A DIFFERENT JOB NOW. TOOK OVER MY DAD'S BUSINESS.

YOU THREW IN THE TOWEL... REALLY?
YOU'RE THE ONE WHO SAID I WOULDN'T MAKE IT.

I ***NEVER*** SAID THAT...
AND WHY THE HELL WOULD YOU LISTEN TO ***ME***, ANYWAY?

UH... BECAUSE I WAS YOUR ***ASSISTANT?***

NO. YOU CAN'T LET ANYONE TELL YOU WHAT YOU CAN BE OR NOT.
I WAS PROBABLY TRYING TO TOUGHEN YOU UP...

...***IF*** I SAID THAT.

...YEAH... OKAY...

He **said** it... I can still hear him saying it ten years later.

That's a memory that sticks with you... The time your favorite artist shat all over your hopes and dreams.
Y'KNOW, IN THE '70S, BENNIE WOULD BE HAVING A BIG PARTY TONIGHT... WITH GIRLS ALREADY PAID FOR.

So it's funny that Hal doesn't remember it at all...
But it's the bitter kind of funny.
THAT'S HOW HE KEPT ALL THOSE INKING GIGS...
GETTING HIS EDITORS LAID.

I guess I could have been any one of a hundred kids whose work he ripped apart over the years.

I start wondering again why Hal asked for ***me*** as his driver...
I'LL BE RIGHT BACK...

But then I see him following Rook Morgan into the *Men's Room*...

And something about that just feels wrong.
??

*Rook Morgan* is another name you won't know.
Rook spent his career doing fill-in issues of books like ***MAN-THING***, ***CAT-LAD***, and ***THE HAUNTED TANK***, and was never anyone's favorite artist.

Years ago he gave an interview where he called Hal his *mentor*...

And Hal had ripped that page out of the magazine and set it on fire.
NO - NO - DON'T!!

TELL ME RIGHT NOW, YOU FAT BASTARD...
HAL - PLEASE...
I DON'T KNOW WHAT YOU'RE TALKING ABOUT...

HAL - CUT IT OUT!

BACK OFF!!
JESUS!

THIS SON OF A BITCH HAS SOMETHING OF MINE...

I DON'T... I DON'T...
I SWEAR TO GOD, I DON'T...

BULLSHIT... YOU TOOK ADVANTAGE OF ME WHEN I WAS SICK...
I SHOULD'VE NEVER LET YOU INTO MY HOUSE...

HAL, PLEASE... IT'S NOT ME... I SWEAR TO YOU.

THEN WHO?

LOOK... I HEARD FROM LUCINDA A FEW WEEKS BACK...
SHE WAS LOOKING TO SELL SOME OF YOUR PAGES, OKAY?

WHY DIDN'T YOU CALL ME?
SHE SAID YOU GAVE THEM TO HER...

AND YOU BELIEVED THAT? WHY, BECAUSE YOU WANT TO FUCK HER?

HEY - YOU KNOW WHAT?
SCREW YOU, HAL.

UP THERE ON YOUR HIGH HORSE...
LIKE YOU NEVER STOLE ANYONE ELSE'S ART.

I kind of respect Rook's nerve for saying that...
OH... YOU SON OF A BITCH...

But he clearly didn't think it through.
KRAKK
AHH - !

You don't throw fuel on a drunken maniac.
COME ON...
WE GOTTA GO - NOW!
...FUUHHH... HH...

HEY... I STILL HAVE A DRINK...
NO, YOU DON'T.

See, back in the '70s, when Hal's gambling debts were destroying his second marriage, he got a bad rep as an art thief.
Pages would go missing from editors' desks and show up on the collectors market.
Wrightson, Kirby, Windsor-Smith... Any name that would sell.
WILL YOU SLOW DOWN? TAKE IT EASY.
I'M TRYING TO GET AWAY FROM HERE BEFORE THE POLICE SHOW UP TO ARREST YOU.

And even though this was an open secret in the industry...
ROOK'S NOT GONNA CALL THE COPS.
YOU BROKE HIS NOSE. THAT'S FELONY ASSAULT.

...No one ever mentioned it to Hal.
HE'S NOT CALLING THE COPS... I'M HIS "MENTOR" REMEMBER?
TRUST ME, HE'LL BE DINING OUT ON THIS STORY FOR YEARS.

Maybe because they all knew how ashamed he was.

YOU WANT TO TELL ME WHAT THAT WAS ABOUT?

YOU HEARD IT ALL... SOMEONE STOLE SOMETHING FROM ME...
LAST YEAR, WHEN I WAS SICK... GUESS I LET MY GUARD DOWN.

AND THIS LUCINDA CHICK, SHE HAS YOUR PAGES?
APPARENTLY...

OKAY... SO WHERE DO WE FIND HER?

Lucinda lived in a little rundown cottage near the beach.
She wasn't home, but Hal knew where to find her...
STILL LETTING THAT LITTLE TYRANT RUN YOUR LIFE, HUH?

HAL?
HEY, BABY...

YOU KNOW, A CALL BEFORE A VISIT IS GENERALLY APPRECIATED...
OR SO I'VE BEEN TOLD.

TOUCHÉ.

WHO'S YOUR LITTLE FRIEND?
I'M JUST THE DRIVER.

JACOB USED TO BE ONE OF MY ASSISTANTS.
AHH... OF COURSE HE DID...

YOU KNOW WHY I'M HERE...

I DO?

OH... OKAY.
AND HERE I WAS THINKING YOU JUST MISSED ME.

DON'T TRY TO MAKE YOURSELF THE VICTIM. YOU STOLE FROM ME.

OH GOD NO... NO ONE CAN EVER BE AS MUCH OF A VICTIM AS YOU... CAN THEY?

WELL, YOU'RE TOO LATE, ANYWAY...
I ALREADY SOLD EVERYTHING.

GOT A DECENT PRICE, TOO. PAID OFF MY MORTGAGE...
JUST LIKE YOU ALWAYS PROMISED YOU WERE GONNA DO.

SO... THANKS FOR THAT, DAD.

NOW... WAS THAT ALL YOU CAME FOR?
BECAUSE MR SNICKERS IS GETTING COLD OUT HERE.

WAIT...

WHAT...?

WHO DID YOU SELL THEM TO?

I was wracking my brains...
Trying to remember Hal ever mentioning a daughter...
ARE YOU OKAY?
YEAH, I JUST NEED A DRINK...

When I got the answer to the question I'd been asking before...
HEY, YOU SAID YOU WENT INTO YOUR FAMILY *BUSINESS*...
YEAH, WHY?

Why Hal had picked *me* to be his driver.
YOUR DAD WAS A *THIEF*, RIGHT?

UHH... WHERE ARE YOU *GOING* WITH THIS, HAL?

WELL... I'M HOPING YOU KNOW SOMEONE WHO LIKES TO BREAK INTO RICH PEOPLE'S HOUSES...

...BECAUSE I NEED YOU TO HELP ME *ROB* SOMEONE.

Saturday

I feel like I'm not giving you a fair picture of Hal Crane.
I'm talking like he's just this string of bad luck and drunken rage... But there was more to him than that.

So let me tell you my favorite memory of Hal.

It was just before Christmas, 1988, and we were pulling an all-nighter finishing a story for *Tomb of Unknown Horror*...

I was filling in blacks, and inking some of the backgrounds - all the boring stuff - and Hal was finishing everything else.

On tight deadlines, it was a nightmare trying to keep up with him.

He was about 60 then, but he could still go *days* without sleep when he was inking...

I'd be running on fumes, and with each page Hal somehow seemed *more* awake... more energized.

We finished around 4:30 in the morning.
I could tell Hal was happy with how this one had turned out and I felt a swell of pride that kind of surprised me.

Then he said -
HEY KID... YOU WANNA SEE SOMETHING?

And he took me down the stairs into his house...

...To his library, which was strictly *off-limits* to assistants.

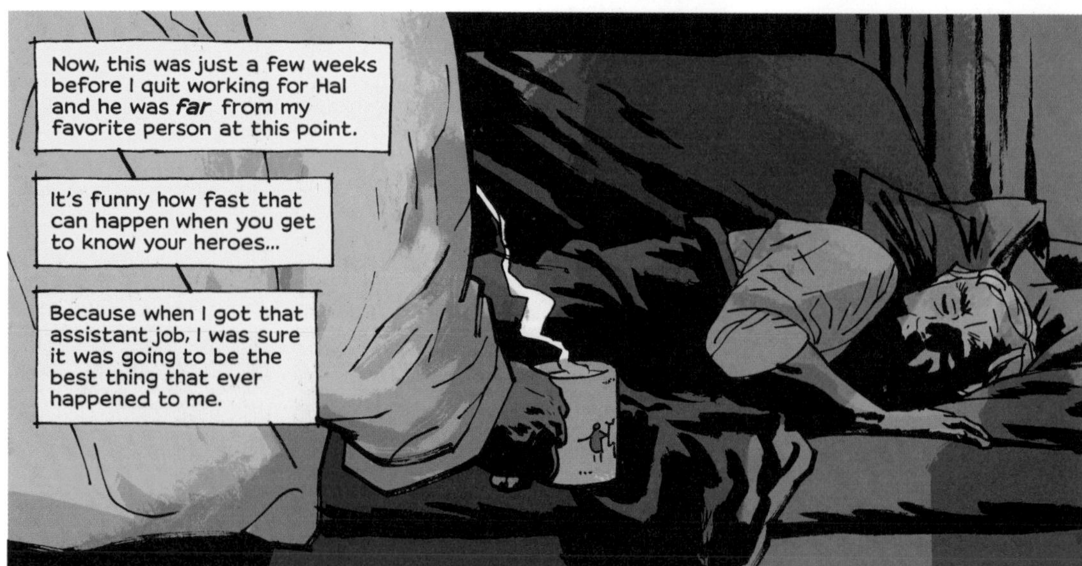
Now, this was just a few weeks before I quit working for Hal and he was *far* from my favorite person at this point.
It's funny how fast that can happen when you get to know your heroes...
Because when I got that assistant job, I was sure it was going to be the best thing that ever happened to me.

See, I'd never done too well with people. I had friends, sure, but even they made me feel anxious and alienated most of the time.
My whole life, my happiest days were the ones I spent alone with my books and comics.
Those were my *real* friends... The ones that helped me escape all the thoughts spinning around in my head.
SNAKE MAN
And from the first time I saw his name in the credits - in *SWORD of the SAVAGE #54* - Hal Crane was one of my favorite artists.
I was always trying to draw like him... Or rereading his *fanzine* interviews from the '60s and '70s.
This was a huge part of my childhood.
I knew he wasn't the same guy from those old interviews when I went to work for him, but I still had stars in my eyes anyway.
I was going to study with the *master*... So what if he was kind of a crotchety old man now? So were all the teachers in *kung fu* movies.
I *KNOW*, MINDY... I'M *SORRY*.
LOOK, I'LL DO MY BEST TO MAKE SURE HE GETS TO THE *AWARDS CEREMONY*, OKAY?
YOUR *BEST* -- ?!

But the reality of Hal wiped those stars away pretty quickly...
If things hadn't been so *screwed up* back at home, I might've quit right away.
Instead I was stuck in a room with a guy I'd grown up worshipping, seeing what was left of him...

The bitter drunken rants about publishers and editors and studio bosses who lied and ripped him off...

The fights with his ex-wives over alimony payments...

Soaking his hands in ice at the end of the day...

I started thinking that a 60-year-old man still having to pull all-nighters was more sad than anything.
IS IT ALL SET?
WE'LL SEE... MY FRIEND'S GONNA MEET US FOR LUNCH...

Anyway, so Hal led me into his library, which was impressive.
Walls lined with art books, old pulp magazines, paperback crime novels right next to great works of literature... Shakespeare, Dickens, Cervantes.

But what he wanted to show me was locked inside a cabinet across the room.
His real treasure...
His newspaper strip collection.
STAR KING

They were big clothbound books, and pasted into them were daily strips and Sunday pages from the comics Hal had loved as a child.
Terry and the Pirates, Jungle Jackson, Scorchy Smith, Captain Easy... and Star King.

My exposure to newspaper strips up until then was pretty limited... and Hal knew that.
So he poured himself a drink and started showing me his favorite sequences... Telling me about the characters...
...SO MAX KING IS A SPACE PILOT WHO GETS PULLED THROUGH A VORTEX INTO ANOTHER GALAXY...

And as he talked, I could see that kid inside of him, still.

The one who carefully cut his favorite strips from the paper every day and glued them into books that he saved for his entire life.

The kid who survived the Depression by disappearing into magic and mystery and tales of wonder.
STAR
KING
By Archie Lewi

It was really something, to see that there was still some joy inside Hal...
Even if it was wistful and nostalgic.
...AND THEN MAX AND PRINCESS LILAH BECAME *SPACE PIRATES* FOR THE NEXT TWO YEARS...

Eventually, he fell asleep while I was looking at one of the books, so I threw a blanket on him and went home...
And the next day it was like none of it had happened.
He was back to treating me like an unwanted stepchild who couldn't even rule *panel borders* correctly.

But still, that's my favorite memory of Hal.

LOOK... JUST FOLLOW MY *LEAD* IN HERE, OKAY?

WE DON'T WANT TO TELL RICKY ANYTHING HE DOESN'T *NEED* TO KNOW.

YOU DON'T *TRUST* HIM?
NO, I *DO*... I JUST...
I *KNOW* HIM, TOO.

...SO WHAT KIND OF BUILDING AM I LOOKING AT?
IS THERE A **DOORMAN** OR A FRONT DESK... OR...?
NOT THAT I RECALL... BUT I WAS ONLY **THERE** ONCE...

OKAY... SO WHAT **DO** YOU RECALL?
I THINK WE CALLED UP FROM THE FRONT DOOR AND HE **BUZZED** US IN...

HE'S ON THE THIRD FLOOR...
APARTMENT **3-G**, LIKE THE COMIC STRIP.
OKAY... THAT'S GOOD.
SHOULD BE NO PROBLEM THEN...

Ricky Lawless was one of those ***friends*** I mentioned before, the ones who made me so anxious.
I'd known him since we were kids, and he'd ***always*** been a thief...
Houses, shops, cars... Ricky didn't care, he'd break into anything.

I was constantly worried he was going to get me arrested as an accomplice, long before I *actually* was one.
SO WHAT AM I LOOKING FOR WHEN I GET INSIDE?
SOME OF MY OLD PAGES, BUT THIS GUY HAS SO MUCH ART, YOU'LL NEVER FIND THEM...

I'LL HAVE TO COME IN AFTER YOU DISABLE HIS ALARM...
WE CAN GO UP THE BACK STAIRS IF THERE'S *CAMERAS* AT THE FRONT.

*YOU'RE* COMING... REALLY?

IT'S NOT *FORT KNOX*... IT'S AN APARTMENT.
WE'LL BE IN AND OUT IN FIVE MINUTES.

SO WHAT'S THE DEAL, THIS GUY'S A *COLLECTOR?* IS HE *RICH?*
YEAH, HE'S PRETTY RICH...
HE WROTE THAT *CHRISTMAS* MOVIE... THE ONE WHERE THE KID PUKES ON SANTA?

OH YEAH, I SAW THE *TRAILER* FOR THAT.
I could practically hear the wheels turning in Ricky's mind now...

And I instantly regretted calling him.
SO LOOK... WHAT IF WE GET UP THERE AND WE CAN'T FIND YOUR SHIT BECAUSE IT'S INSIDE SOME SAFE?

OH... YEAH... I GUESS THAT'S *POSSIBLE*...

WE DON'T WANT TO GO TO ALL THIS EFFORT TO HIT A BRICK WALL, Y'KNOW?

SO, *WHAT*... YOU DON'T WANT TO DO IT?

NO, I WANT TO DO IT *RIGHT NOW*, WHILE THE GUY'S STILL *HOME*...
SO I CAN GET HIM TO OPEN HIS FUCKING *SAFE*.
Of course he would make it more dangerous...
That was who he was.

The problem with Ricky was that his dad had been a legend, and not in a good way.
WHO IS IT?
UPS... GOT A PACKAGE FOR A DAVID MANDRILL...
I NEED A SIGNATURE.

And when he was killed, Ricky started changing...
BZZZZ

Trying to prove to the world he was just as fearless as his dad had been.

And maybe he was now, but I still remembered the kid he used to be, who was always "borrowing" my comics...

Who pressured me into my first counterfeiting job, making us fake passes for Comic Fest.

Back then, we'd stay up all night in the movie room...

...And search the *quarter bins.*

He loved that convention just like I did, even though he was embarrassed to admit it.

But that kid was gone now.
KNNK KNK
3-G

All grown up and reckless.
HOLY SHIT -- !

LET'S KEEP THAT VOICE DOWN, OKAY?

ALL RIGHT, OLD MAN, HAVE A LOOK AROUND... IT'S ALL CLEAR.
WHERE'S THE GUY?
WHAT'D YOU *DO* TO HIM?

RELAX... HE'S IN HERE...

*SEE?*
IS SOMEONE ELSE *THERE?*

SHUT UP, *DAVE.*

THE SAFE'S IN A WALK-IN CLOSET DOWN HERE... BUNCH OF ART AND STUFF IN THERE...
COUPLE ENVELOPES OF CASH, BUT I HAVEN'T COUNTED THEM YET.

WE'RE NOT HERE FOR HIS *MONEY.*
MAYBE *YOU* AREN'T...

GOD DAMN IT...
WHERE ARE THEY...

HANG ON -
*HERE* WE GO.

OH, WHAT THE *FUCK?!*

WHAT IS IT?
JUST SOME SHIT I DID IN THE *'70S*...
*NOT* WHAT I WAS LOOKING FOR.

I NEED TO TALK TO *DAVID*...
UH... THAT'S NOT SUCH A GREAT IDEA, MAN...

I DON'T CARE.

HEY... WHAT'S GOING ON...?

HAL? YOU BROKE INTO MY HOUSE?

YOU BOUGHT SOME PAGES FROM MY DAUGHTER.
THEY WERE STOLEN AND I WANT THEM BACK.
GIVE THE MAN WHAT HE WANTS, DAVE.

HAL, YOU KNOW - I WOULD NEVER -
HE DOESN'T CARE. WHERE'S THE STUFF?

IN THE SAFE! THEY'RE IN THE SAFE!

IT'S YOUR FIRST ZANGAR STORY... I HAVEN'T GOTTEN IT FRAMED YET BUT -
THAT'S ALL THAT SHE SOLD YOU?

CAN HE PLEASE STOP AIMING THAT AT ME?

ARE YOU TELLING THE TRUTH?
YES!!

WELL... SHIT.

We untie David Mandrill and Ricky convinces him it's better if he just **forgets** this little burglary ever happened...
I don't trust it, but the idea of Ricky coming back someday clearly scares the shit out of him.
He even apologizes to Hal as we're leaving.
...YOU KNOW HOW **CHARLES DICKENS** FIRST GOT FAMOUS...?
ON THE BACK OF A **CARTOONIST**.

ROBERT SEYMOUR WAS SO POPULAR THAT HIS PUBLISHER WANTED TO PUT OUT A **MONTHLY MAGAZINE** OF HIS DRAWINGS...
THEY JUST NEEDED A **HACK WRITER** TO TAKE HIS ART AND ADD SOME WORDS.

HELL... DICKENS WASN'T EVEN THEIR **FIRST CHOICE**.

BUT WHAT DOES HE **DO?** HE TAKES OVER THE WHOLE ENTERPRISE...

STARTS MAKING SEYMOUR DRAW WHAT **HE** WANTS HIM TO, GIVING HIM TONS OF NOTES...
THE USUAL **WRITER** BULLSHIT...

IT WAS THE MAN'S **DREAM** GIG... AND SUDDENLY IT'S A NIGHTMARE...

SEYMOUR BLEW HIS OWN *BRAINS* OUT BEFORE HE EVEN FINISHED THE SECOND ISSUE...
AND DICKENS WENT ON TO FAME AND FORTUNE... AND *IMMORTALITY*.
Hal was drinking away his disappointment, so of course it was time for the Dickens speech... I'd heard it before.

Pretty soon he'd get to Jack Cole... And poor Joe Shuster... Maybe even Archie Lewis...

Comics' *casualties*... A long line that he must've been certain he'd be joining...

Like he felt its gravity pulling him in.

HEY, MAYBE WE SHOULD CLOSE THE TAB HERE...
WHAT... *WHY?*

I GOTTA GET YOU BACK TO YOUR HOTEL IF YOU'RE GONNA *CHANGE* BEFORE THE CEREMONY...
AHH... I DON'T KNOW ABOUT THAT THING...

NO. HAL, YOU ARE NOT SKIPPING THE AWARDS SHOW.
MINDY WILL KILL ME... SERIOUSLY.
COME ON, KID... WHAT DOES IT MATTER, REALLY?
AN AWARD FOR SPENDING MY ENTIRE LIFE BENT OVER A DRAWING TABLE...

...WITH NOTHING TO SHOW FOR IT, JUST LIKE EVERY OTHER GUY THEY SCREWED...

YOU KNOW WHAT WALLY WOOD SAID?
HERE WE GO...

HE SAID IF HE HAD TO DO IT ALL OVER AGAIN, HE'D CUT OFF HIS OWN GODDAMN HANDS...

I DON'T KNOW, MAN...

I NEVER WATCHED THAT STUPID CARTOON YOU MADE, BUT I ALWAYS DUG YOUR COMICS.
EVEN MY DAD LIKED THOSE ISSUES OF ZANGAR YOU DREW...

YOU KNOW I WROTE THE STORY FOR THOSE TOO... BUT MARV CHANGED ALL THE DIALOG AND FUCKED IT UP.
AND YOU'RE STILL PISSED ABOUT IT TWENTY YEARS LATER... OBVIOUSLY YOU CARE, HAL.
JUST GO ACCEPT THE AWARD.

I'M NOT GETTING UP THERE AND PLAYING NICE SO THE PUBLISHERS CAN FEEL GOOD ABOUT THEMSELVES...
LIKE THIS RACKET ISN'T A RACKET...

SO THEN DON'T, MAN...
GO UP THERE AND SHIT ALL OVER THEM.

HELL, I'D EVEN GO WATCH THAT... IT'D BE AMAZING.

WAIT -- WOULD I HAVE TO PUT ON A SUIT?

YEAH... IF YOU'RE GONNA SIT AT MY TABLE, YOU DO.

To Ricky's credit, he did convince the old bastard to actually *go* to the event he'd been flown out here for...
But remember what I said before about not throwing fuel on a drunken maniac?

And Hal kept drinking right through the ceremony, of course... While I just felt this creeping sense of doom.

All these old "friends" stopping over to say hi had no idea what they were in for... That they were about to become part of the legend of Hal Crane.
GREAT TO SEEYA, HAL...
*THANKS,* WILL.

By the time Mindy comes to get him for his award, my nerves are so bad that I'm drinking the hard stuff, too.

And Ricky's just... amused, by all of it.
Keeps leaning over to ask me who people *are* when they win.

Then, right before they call them up to the stage, I see Hal and his old boss *Frank Harmony* talking...
And they look like two *old pals* burying the hatchet.

Hal lets Frank pat him on the shoulder a few times and they even shake hands.

But when Frank gets up to introduce him...
...TO SAY HE'S A GENIUS, THAT HE WAS NEARLY WITHOUT PEER... IS NOT ENOUGH...

...Hal just *glares*...
NO, THE MAN WE HONOR *TONIGHT* IS ONE OF THE BEST TO EVER PUT PEN TO BOARD...

And I know what's coming next is going to be really ugly.
...SO PLEASE HELP ME WELCOME A *TRUE* GRANDMASTER OF THE ART FORM... *HAL CRANE*.

But maybe the applause surprises him... Or the standing ovation.
Because whatever he was planning to say...
Whatever dirt he was going to bring up...

He doesn't.
Instead, he clears his throat, and he gives the acceptance speech everyone in the room really wants to hear...
He talks about growing up reading the funnies... Dreaming of a life in four-color newsprint.

He talks about how lucky he was to be mentored by so many great artists...
And how much luckier still, that he got to spend fifty years doing the thing he loved most in the world.

I almost can't believe it.

And even Ricky Lawless seems touched.

But then... as the crowd is applauding him again...

Hal turns around and ***breaks*** Frank Harmony's jaw...
KRAAAK

Ricky's laughter is the only thing I can hear above the chaos that follows...

As the whole room goes nuts trying to get to the stage.

And somehow - stupidly - I manage to put ***myself*** between Hal and Frank's security man...

...Who has a ***taser***.
GA -- AAHH -- !

BCPD
BCPD
BCPD
SO... GOOD SPEECH, I GUESS.
THANKS.

WHAT HAPPENED...?
IT LOOKED LIKE YOU AND FRANK WERE MENDING FENCES.

WE WERE... HE OFFERED ME FIFTY GRAND AS A BONUS, FOR THAT NEW PRINCESS YAZ SHOW.

THAT'S GREAT... ISN'T IT?

Pfft... A "BONUS."
WHAT A PRICK.

HEY, DID YOU REALLY QUIT DRAWING?
YOU WERE GOOD... YOU SHOULD STICK WITH IT.

I THOUGHT YOU SAID COMICS WAS DYING?

COMICS HAVE BEEN DYING SINCE 1954, KID...
DON'T LET THAT STOP YOU...

This, right here, was my favorite moment of the weekend...

And I probably should've left it at that... Just stopped talking.

But I had to ask the question...
SO WHAT WERE THOSE PAGES YOU WERE LOOKING FOR?

SOME STUFF I DREW BACK WHEN I WAS WORKING FOR ARCHIE LEWIS...
DON'T WORRY ABOUT IT...

IT'S JUST A MISTAKE I MADE... ONE OF MANY, RIGHT?
BUT I WANTED TO KEEP THIS ONE TO MYSELF...

IT'S HARD TO EXPLAIN.

I just had to be sure.
YEAH, OKAY...

Sunday

See, someone once referred to Hal Crane as "a master without a masterpiece" but that wasn't actually true...

There *was* a masterpiece, it's just that only a handful of people had ever seen it...
And only on Hal's most drunken, self-pitying nights.
That's when he got *confessional*... When he told you his secrets.

Like the *real story* of Archie Lewis's death.

I can still hear his voice, cracking with emotion... As he brought these pages out to show me...
STAR KING

Hal had only been inking backgrounds on *STAR KING* for a month or two when the syndicate approached him.
Archie was demanding a raise and a piece of ownership, so they figured it was time to put the old man out to pasture.
And they wanted Hal to take over the strip, if they liked his *samples*.
So for the next month, Hal worked his day job, then stayed up late into the night putting together eight weeks of dailies and Sundays.
He knew he should have hated himself for what he was doing to Archie, but he didn't.
In fact, he'd never been happier in his life.
Even the writing came easy, as if *Max King* and *Princess Lilah* themselves were telling him what happened next.
He told himself maybe Archie would be happy it was someone like him who took over...
Someone who really knew and loved the strip... Who could do it justice...
If he could just show Archie his pages, maybe he wouldn't see them as a betrayal.
But Hal knew that wasn't true... and when someone at the agency tipped off Archie, he took Hal for a ride and drove straight into a wall.

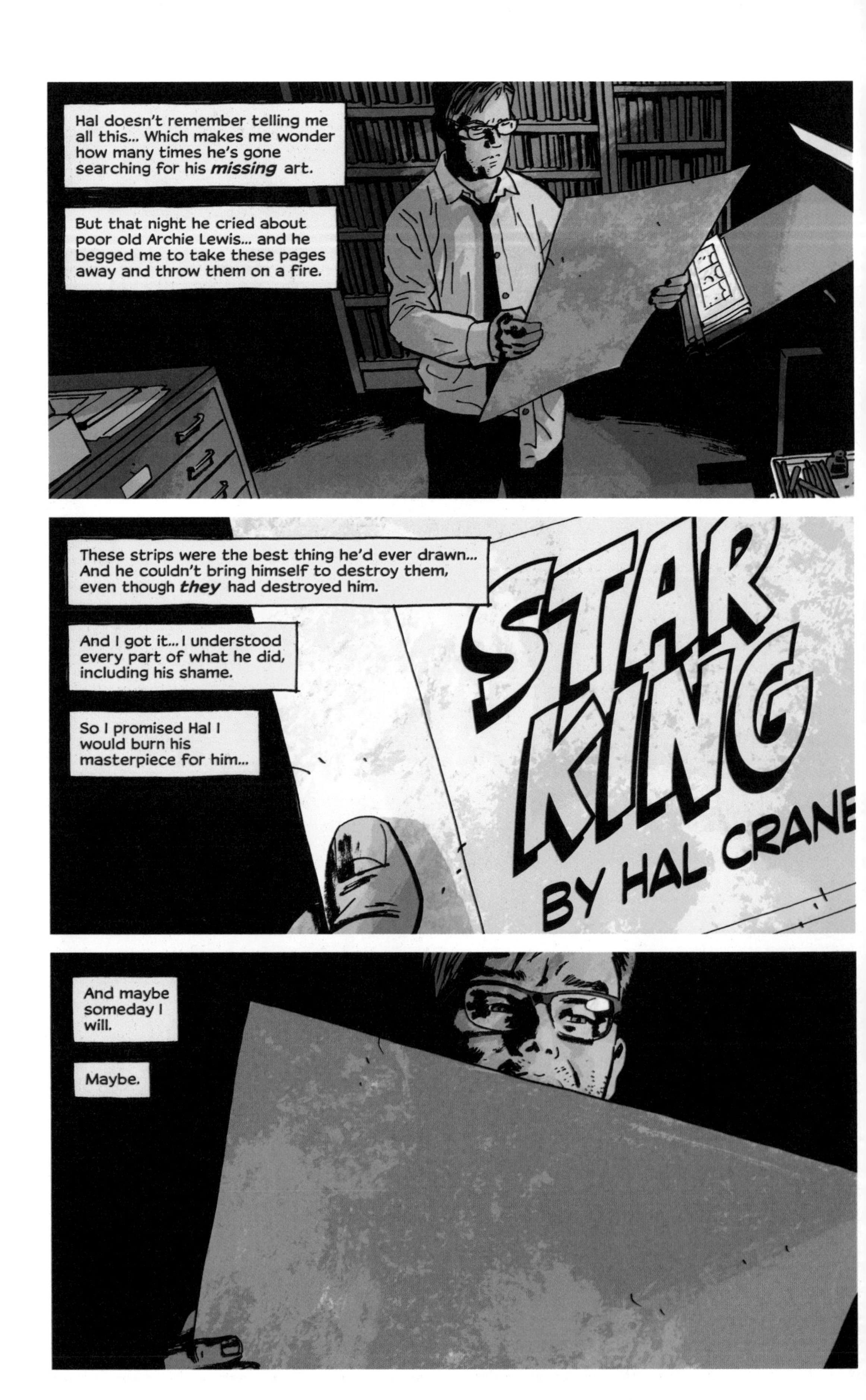
Hal doesn't remember telling me all this... Which makes me wonder how many times he's gone searching for his *missing* art.
But that night he cried about poor old Archie Lewis... and he begged me to take these pages away and throw them on a fire.
These strips were the best thing he'd ever drawn... And he couldn't bring himself to destroy them, even though *they* had destroyed him.
STAR KING
BY HAL CRANE
And I got it... I understood every part of what he did, including his shame.
So I promised Hal I would burn his masterpiece for him...
And maybe someday I will.
Maybe.

## BIOGRAPHIES

Ed Brubaker is one of the most award-winning writers in comics. His bestselling titles with Sean Phillips, CRIMINAL, INCOGNITO, FATALE, THE FADE OUT, MY HEROES HAVE ALWAYS BEEN JUNKIES and KILL OR BE KILLED have been translated around the world to great acclaim, and Marvel's movies featuring his co-creation, The Winter Soldier, have all been international blockbusters. Ed lives in Los Angeles, where he works in comics, film, and television, most recently on HBO's *Westworld* and as the co-creator and writer of Amazon's *Too Young To Die* with Nicolas Winding Refn.

Drawing comics professionally since the age of fifteen, Eisner Award-winning Sean Phillips has worked for all the major publishers. Since drawing *Sleeper, Hellblazer, Batman, X-Men, Marvel Zombies*, and Stephen King's *The Dark Tower*, Sean has concentrated on creator-owned books including CRIMINAL, KILL OR BE KILLED, INCOGNITO, FATALE, MY HEROES HAVE ALWAYS BEEN JUNKIES and THE FADE OUT.

He is currently drawing a new volume of the long-running CRIMINAL written by his long-time collaborator Ed Brubaker and coloured by his son Jacob Phillips.

He lives in the Lake District in the UK.

Jacob Phillips is a freelance illustrator based in Manchester, England. When he was just 11 years old he wrote, drew and home-printed his first comic book, *Roboy*. He took this to Brighton Comic Convention and flogged it from behind a table, selling out on the first day. Ever since, he has been scribbling away, working with clients such as BBC, Arrow Film, Headspace Property, Arte and Kino Lorber. Jacob is the current colorist on Ed Brubaker and Sean Phillips' CRIMINAL as well as working as a freelance illustrator and comic book artist.

**OTHER BOOKS BY BRUBAKER AND PHILLIPS:**

| | |
|---|---|
| CRIMINAL: Coward | ISBN: 978-1-63215-170-4 |
| CRIMINAL: Lawless | ISBN: 978-1-63215-203-9 |
| CRIMINAL: The Dead And The Dying | ISBN: 978-1-63215-233-6 |
| CRIMINAL: Bad Night | ISBN: 978-1-63215-260-2 |
| CRIMINAL: The Sinners | ISBN: 978-1-63215-298-5 |
| CRIMINAL: The Last Of The Innocent | ISBN: 978-1-63215-299-2 |
| CRIMINAL: Wrong Time, Wrong Place | ISBN: 978-1-63215-877-2 |
| CRIMINAL The Deluxe Edition Volume One | ISBN: 978-1-5343-0541-0 |
| CRIMINAL The Deluxe Edition Volume Two | ISBN: 978-1-5343-0543-4 |
| FATALE The Deluxe Edition Volume One | ISBN: 978-1-60706-942-3 |
| FATALE The Deluxe Edition Volume Two | ISBN: 978-1-63215-503-0 |
| FATALE Book One: Death Chases Me | ISBN: 978-1-60706-563-0 |
| FATALE Book Two: The Devil's Business | ISBN: 978-1-60706-618-7 |
| FATALE Book Three: West Of Hell | ISBN: 978-1-60706-743-6 |
| FATALE Book Four: Pray For Rain | ISBN: 978-1-60706-835-8 |
| FATALE Book Five: Curse The Demon | ISBN: 978-1-63215-007-3 |
| THE FADE OUT | ISBN: 978-1-5343-0860-2 |
| THE FADE OUT Deluxe Edition | ISBN: 978-1-63215-911-3 |
| KILL OR BE KILLED Volume One | ISBN: 978-1-5343-0028-6 |
| KILL OR BE KILLED Volume Two | ISBN: 978-1-5343-0228-0 |
| KILL OR BE KILLED Volume Three | ISBN: 978-1-5343-0471-0 |
| KILL OR BE KILLED Volume Four | ISBN: 978-1-5343-0651-6 |
| MY HEROES HAVE ALWAYS BEEN JUNKIES | ISBN: 978-1-5343-0846-6 |